Whiskers, Once and Always

ALSO BY DORIS ORGEL

My War with Mrs. Galloway

WHISKERS
ONCE AND ALWAYS

BY DORIS ORGEL

Illustrated by Carol Newsom

Viking Kestrel

VIKING KESTREL

Viking Penguin Inc., 40 West 23rd Street, New York, New York 10010, U.S.A.
Penguin Books Ltd, Harmondsworth, Middlesex, England
Penguin Books Australia Ltd, Ringwood, Victoria, Australia
Penguin Books Canada Limited, 2801 John Street, Markham, Ontario, Canada L3R 1B4
Penguin Books (N.Z.) Ltd, 182–190 Wairau Road, Auckland 10, New Zealand

Text copyright © Doris Orgel, 1986
Illustrations copyright © Carol Newsom, 1986
All rights reserved

First published in 1986 by Viking Penguin Inc.
Published simultaneously in Canada

Printed in U.S.A. by
Haddon Craftsmen, Bloomsberg, Pennsylvania
Set in Sabon Roman
1   2   3   4   5   90   89   88   87   86

LIBRARY OF CONGRESS CATALOGING IN PUBLICATION DATA
Orgel, Doris.   Whiskers, once and always
Summary: When her beloved cat Whiskers dies, Rebecca finds it
difficult at first to vent her anger and accept her mother's comfort.
[1. Death—Fiction. 2. Cats—Fiction] I. Title.
PZ7.O632Wg 1986   [Fic]   86-5468   ISBN 0-670-80959-4

For my Bobbie   D. O.

Contents

Whiskers, Once and Always

Pow!

I punched Jason Abeloff, really hard, *pow*! Because of what he said to me. Just when my fist crashed into his nose, Ms. Field, our teacher, walked in.

"Becky, I am shocked!" she said. "I can almost not believe it!"

I could almost not believe it myself. I'd never punched anybody before. Oh, maybe Michael a couple of times. But just on the arm. Just in fun . . .

"Jason, what did you do to Becky?" asked Ms. Field.

"Nothing. Honest! I didn't even touch her!"

"Is that true, Becky?"

"Yes—"

Then I saw the blood. It ran down Jason's mouth and chin, onto his shirt. His shirt had a picture of Dracula on it. The Dracula's forehead and big long teeth had blood, real blood, on them. Jason said, "Oh, no! It's my favorite shirt!"

Ms. Field grabbed a bunch of Kleenex and held them to his nose. "Somebody go to the nurse's office, quick, and bring an ice bag!"

I offered to.

"Not you, Becky. You stay right here."

She sent Melanie for the ice bag. She sat Jason down and held the ice bag to the back of his neck, and she made him squeeze his nose together and only breathe through his mouth. Finally his nose stopped bleeding.

"Now, everybody take your seats," said Ms. Field. "Except Becky Suslow. You have some explaining to do." And she asked me, "Why did you punch Jason?"

"Um, because—" I hardly ever have trouble getting words out. But I just stood there with my mouth open, like a dope. Like I'd forgotten how to talk.

"Because, what? Out with it, Becky. I don't have all day."

"Um, Jason said something—" My face got all hot.

"I am waiting," said Ms. Field. "What did he say?"

Something terrible. I could sooner have told Ms. Field what's written on the girls' room walls than what Jason said.

Everybody waited, held their breath. Our classroom was so quiet, you could have heard a goldfish swim.

Clannng! The bell rang, so loud it jangled right through my bones.

"All right, Becky, go sit down." Ms. Field started to take attendance: "Abeloff, Baker, Canillo, Chavez—" When she came to Suslow, she said, "Report to me at recess."

At recess I stood by her desk. Looking through the window, I could see the oak tree in the playground. And I could see the ball in the air when somebody threw it high.

Ms. Field said, "I can't understand it. You're usually so sensible and well-behaved in school. What could have made you do such a thing? Are you ready to explain it to me now?"

"I can't, Ms. Field. I just can't."

"Why not? It couldn't have been *that* bad."

Yes, it was. Even just thinking about it made the awful picture come back on inside my mind. I was scared that if I told it, the picture would stay stuck in my mind forever.

Ms. Field tapped her pencil on the desk. Tap, tap. "Well, if you can't tell me, you'll have to go to you-know-who."

Mr. Bruzzo. The "Brute." The principal of our school.

When we have assembly, and when he visits classrooms, he always says there's more to being a principal than just punishing kids, and we shouldn't be scared of him. But the only time kids get sent to his office is when they've gotten in trouble. And he's big, like a buffalo. His chest bulges out. His voice booms, deep and loud. He clomps when he walks down the hall. You can hear him from far away. And when kids come out of his office, they have a funny look on their faces, and won't even say what happened in there . . .

One thing everyone knows that happens when you have to go to Mr. Bruzzo: He calls up your parents, and one of them has to come to school.

Well, my father lives in Portland, Oregon, three thousand miles away. So it would be my mother. Oh, wow. I can just see the look on her face!

Mom's a doctor. She works in a hospital. Some days she's so busy, she doesn't even take a lunch break. She just eats her sandwich or her yogurt and fruit while she's seeing patients.

Ms. Field knows this. She said, "Let's save your mother the trouble. Let's just keep this between us." And she asked me again, "What did Jason say?"

I decided I'd make myself tell it. Quick, I'd get it over with. "He said that I—" Uh-oh! The picture lit up sharp and clear in my mind of everybody with their handkerchiefs out, acting extra nice to me . . .

Ms. Field touched my forehead. "Becky, are you feeling all right?"

I nodded.

"Is anything wrong, other than what happened with Jason? Did something happen at home?"

Yes, yes, yes, and how! But I shook my head. Because if I'd told her, I'd have cried a whole river, and I never could have stopped.

Ms. Field wrinkled her forehead. She opened up her teachers' book. "I've spent all the time I can on this. Now, I have work to do. I'll tell you what: If you can't say it to me, maybe you can write it down. Why don't you try?"

I knew I couldn't. Not in a million years. I sat down in my seat. I looked out the window at the playground tree.

"You'd better start," said Ms. Field.

I started to draw the top part of the tree. It looked bare. I got a big longing to put a cat on one of its branches. I know how to draw cats pretty well. I learned when I was little. I started to draw the head and ears—no, better not. I balled up the paper.

Ms. Field looked my way. She thought I'd been writing. "Better start over. There's not much time left."

When recess was over, I didn't have anything to hand in to her.

She got mad. "Very well, then write it at home. In ink, if you please. No less than two pages. I want a full explanation. And have your mother sign it. If it's not on my desk tomorrow morning, you'll go to Mr. Bruzzo. Is that clear?"

When Everything Was Still Okay

Last Wednesday everything was still okay. It's less than a week, but it seems like ages ago. I didn't have a worry in the world. Mom and I were sitting in our blue-velvet armchair in the foyer, having our special time together, reading *Millions of Cats*. That's a book for little kids but I still like it. So does Mom.

Whiskers lay stretched out across our laps. She must have spent extra time polishing herself up during the day. Her black fur looked especially shiny. The white parts—her paws, tail tip, and a patch under her throat—looked like snow. Her head was on my lap, her tail on Mom's lap. Her whisker hairs touched the inside of my arm. That's a delicious feeling. And she purred.

Purring is amazing. Only cats can do it. Just exactly how they do it, nobody knows.

We came to the last page and recited the ending together:

> *"'Hundreds of cats,*
> *Thousands of cats,*
> *Millions and billions and trillions of cats.'"*

Mom and I rubbed our noses together in rhythm with those words, and we laughed, just like when I was little.

Whiskers gave us a look with her green-golden eyes. Don't human beings act silly sometimes? She took an elegant leap down off our laps, and headed for my room, swinging her tail as she went. She was so light, and so fast on her paws!

Next day, Melanie Rosen, Kyra Farris and I

got together at Melanie's house after school. The three of us are best friends this year.

We finished our science report about meteors and comets. Melanie and Kyra both thought I should do the cover. I used black construction paper and streaked it with dark blue and purple, to make it look like a night sky. I made the meteors orangeish, the comets pale yellow with light green and white tails. The tails should have looked more silvery. But there was no silver crayon.

Right in the middle, Melanie's father came in. I feel kind of nervous around him because he's a rabbi and Mom and I hardly ever go to temple. Melanie says that's dumb, he doesn't keep track of who shows up in temple. He thinks that's everyone's own business. Well, but still, when he was looking over my shoulder, I let the crayon slip, and one comet's tail streaked right off the paper.

Rabbi Rosen thought it was on purpose. He said, "That's a great looking comet, Becky."

When he went out of the room we all piled on the top bunk of Melanie's bunk beds. Kyra

dangled her hair ribbon down to lure Melanie's cats, Ming and Tang, to come on up.
And we played Cats' Castle. The top bunk
was the castle. The bottom bunk was the dun-
geon for captives. For captives we used Melanie's old dolls, and her little brother Josh
when he nagged that we had to let him play.
The floor was the moat, where moat monsters
lived (Josh's plastic alligator collection). Ming
and Tang were Cat Princess and Prince, and
Melanie, Kyra and I took turns being Queen.

Mom picked me up at six on her way from
work.

Usually Mrs. Galloway starts dinner for us.
On Mrs. Galloway's days off, we have pizza
or soup and sandwiches. But Mom said she
felt like having something more delicious, so
she'd stopped off at the butcher's near the
hospital and bought chicken cutlets. What
would I say to Chicken Naomi?

That's a recipe she made up. I said, "Sounds
good to me."

When we got home, only Debbie came to

the door. She wove in and out between our feet, and rubbed her tail against our legs. She learned that from Whiskers, her mother.

I stooped down and stroked along her back, up her tail. "Hey, Debbie, where's your mom?"

I figured that Whiskers was either in my sweater drawer, snoozing, or up on the refrigerator, purring along with the humming it makes. Those were two of her favorite places. Or, maybe she'd gone out . . .

The Yowl

Mom and I have had many talks about in-
door cats and outdoor cats. Mom says if you
live in a big city you owe it to your cats to
keep them in on account of all the traffic, and
getting lost, and other troubles they can get
into out on the streets.

So we always tried our best to keep Whiskers home. But sometimes she'd squeeze out,
even if the window was just open a crack. I
figured if she went to the trouble of making

herself that small, she must have wanted to get out really badly. After all, everybody needs a change of scene once in a while. And probably she had cat friends in the neighborhood, and they had a good time when they got together. She was always in a very good mood when she came home again.

Mom put potatoes in a pot to boil. She got out the wooden mallet to pound the chicken cutlets nice and flat. I opened a can of Salmon Dinner, Whiskers' favorite. I opened the kitchen window wide, so she could smell it if she was anywhere nearby. Debbie came running in from the foyer. I was sure Whiskers would come leaping home, any minute.

Mom started pounding the cutlets.

Uh-oh, the doorbell!

Mom and I looked at each other. I giggled. I was sure it was Mrs. Mean Mouth Nagel. She lives below us. She hates any little noise. Sometimes when Michael comes over, and we so much as take one jump, or bounce a very little ball on the floor, she bangs on her ceiling with a broomstick and yells, "Stop that racket!" One time she came up and complained to Mom, "What's going on here, are you knocking the walls down?" And all Mom was doing was pounding cutlets for Chicken Naomi.

"Becca, you go see who it is." Mom was starting the breading.

I went to the door.

It wasn't Mrs. Nagel. It was the super, Mr. Riordan. He asked, "Is your mother home?"

He was carrying something. It was wrapped in a gray towel. One of the lightbulbs in the hall had burned out and I couldn't see that well.

Mr. Riordan came into our foyer.

Then I saw. It was Whiskers under the towel. Her breath came in fast little spurts. I started to take her. She let out this awful yowl, as if she thought I was going to hurt her. The yowl went through me, like a sharpness, like something was about to start hurting me, a lot, but I didn't know where yet.

Mom came.

Mr. Riordan said, "I was checking the gar-
bage cans out in back. That's where I found
her, Dr. Suslow. She was lying with her leg
out, kind of stiff. Maybe she broke it. Looks
to me like she took a fall off of some-
where."

The roof of our apartment house? That's
where Mom and I first found her. She came
right to us, like she'd found us, and was
choosing us for her humans. Our building is
nine stories high. Too high for a cat to want
to jump down from. Something must have
driven her to it, forced her over the edge. A
gang of enemy cats, maybe. Or some big slob-
bering ferocious dog.

I felt sick to my stomach. Things in the
foyer started whirling around. I imagined fall-
ing through the air. Did the ground come up
at her?

Mom put her hands on my shoulders.

Mr. Riordan said in a cheery voice, "Cats
are tough. Whiskers will be okay, I'll bet you
anything."

Mom thanked him and took her. She let out that awful yowl again.

Mom carried her into her bedroom, laid her down on the bed, took her pulse, listened to her heart with the stethoscope, examined her all over. Then she said, "Everything seems okay, except this knee." Mom put her finger there, very lightly. Whiskers went *Fawwwgh*. She'd never done that to Mom before. And she started to show her claws. But she didn't have the strength to scratch.

Mom soothed her and stroked her. "You poor, poor thing." After a while Whiskers' breathing slowed down to normal.

"Her knee may be broken. Or dislocated," said Mom.

"How will you be able to tell?"

"Only from X-rays."

So then I thought Mom would call up Dr. Ramirez, the vet who gave Whiskers and Debbie their shots, and make an appointment with her. But Mom said, "What Whiskers needs most right now is rest."

And something to drink, I thought. I brought her a saucer of milk. She didn't want any. Then water. She didn't want that either. Not even from the glass with the stem that I taught her to drink from when we first got her. Finally she took one drop of water from my finger.

Mom said, "Don't force it. Just let her be."

Debbie came in. She got ready to jump up on the bed.

"No, Debbie." I caught her. "Your mom needs to rest. Don't bother her just now."

Debbie squirmed out of my arms and went out of the room. She moves like a cat ballerina, as if to some music inside herself. I don't know if she realized anything was wrong with Whiskers.

"See if Debbie's eating," Mom said.

So I went in the kitchen. "Finish your dinner, Deb."

I checked the potatoes and turned off the flame under them.

When I went back into Mom's room Mom

was on the phone. I said, "The potatoes got all mushy."

Mom said, "I'll be right there." And she waved her arm, meaning, Go out, shut the door.

I figured she was talking to Dr. Ramirez.

She stayed on the phone a long time. Finally she came into the kitchen. I asked, "Well? What did she say?"

"What did who say?"

"Dr. Ramirez. Isn't that who you were talking to?"

"No. Dr. Ramirez doesn't even live in Brooklyn anymore! She's moved away to New Jersey." This funny look came over Mom's face. I can't describe it. I've seen it a lot, lately. She was standing right by the stove, only about a foot away from me. But that look on her face made me feel like I was all alone in the kitchen. She said, "I was talking to Pete."

Pete? All that time? While Whiskers was so hurt? While I was worrying my head off?

Pete is this guy Mom's been seeing, Dr. Petrushak. Pete is his nickname. His real first name is Voytek, or something like that.

Mom took the potato masher and glomped it down on the potatoes without draining off the water.

"Ooo, yuk."

Mom frowned. She hates it when I say things like "Yuk." Well, *I* hate watery mashed potatoes. Though, to be honest, I wasn't looking forward to the Chicken Naomi anymore, either.

Mom said, "Pete thinks we're doing the right thing letting her rest. She may feel a lot better by morning."

I asked, "What if she doesn't?"

Mom said, "We'll cross that bridge if we come to it." That look was back, so I knew the next word out of her mouth would be "Pete."

And it was. She said, "Pete says cats are often their own best vets."

Who cared? What did he know about Whiskers? He never even met her! I stomped out of the kitchen. I gave the swinging door such a push it swung back and forth on its own.

Mom called, "Come back and eat your dinner."

I went in to Whiskers.

"How are you doing, Whiskeroo, best cat in the whole world?" I whispered all my pet names for her into her pretty pink ear with the soft white hairs sticking up. She just lay there, very still. The only movement was her breathing. I wanted her to look at me! So I touched her cheek. Then she did, but only with half-open eyes. Her eyes were hazy. There was a mist over them. She gave no sign of being glad to see me. It didn't matter to her one way or the other that I was in the room.

When it was bedtime I asked Mom if Whiskers could spend the night in my sweater drawer.

Mom was still miffed about how I'd stormed out of the kitchen. But she said, "Okay."

She wouldn't let me move her by myself.

She brought the big wooden breadboard and slid it under Whiskers like a stretcher.

"You hold on to her while I carry her. It's important not to jar her."

We got her into the bureau drawer that way. I put in one of her old toys, a chewed-up rubber mouse, in case she started feeling better during the night and wanted to play with something. I covered her with my navy-blue angora sweater, the softest one I have. I kissed her good night on the tip of her nose.

How Things Were
with Whiskers

Next morning Whiskers drank almost half an ounce of milk. Her eyes seemed a little brighter. She was still very quiet, though.

I said, "Mom, can I stay home and watch her?"

But Mrs. Galloway doesn't come till afternoon and Mom doesn't like me to stay alone that long. Mom said no, I had to go to school.

Mrs. Galloway doesn't approve of cat hairs

all over my sweaters. So I wrote her a note. "Dear Mrs. G., Whiskers is not feeling well. Please let her stay in my sweater drawer, just this once." And Mom added all kinds of things she was asking Mrs. G. to buy for dinner, because Pete was coming over that evening, oh wow.

On the way to school I told Michael, my friend in the building, "Something's wrong with Whiskers. Mom thinks she broke her knee. Or dislocated it."

"Dislocated? You mean she left it someplace, and now she can't find it?" Michael thought that was a riot, ha, ha, ha. He squatted down on the sidewalk and looked under a car. "No knee under there. Anyone seen a spare knee anywhere?"

"Cut it out, Michael. 'Dislocated' means when bones are knocked out of their right position, and it can hurt a lot." I explained it to him the way Mom explained it to me. "If it doesn't get better, she may need an operation."

So then Michael calmed down. "Gee, I hope not."

Thank goodness for my other friends, Melanie and Kyra. They know right away when something's the matter.

They were waiting for me by the cubbies. We usually hang out there till the bell rings.

Melanie can make you feel better just by looking at you with her big dark serious eyes. She told me, "The same thing once happened to Ming. We were in the country and she climbed up this really tall tree. I think she didn't mean to jump all the way down, just to another branch. But she missed. Anyway, it shook up her insides. She acted all mopey and wouldn't eat, and just lay in the laundry basket, not even purring or anything."

"Did you have to take her for X-rays?"

Mel said, "No, we were going to, but then she got okay again."

And Kyra had a thin silver necklace with a tiny silver four-leaf clover on it that she always wears. Well, she took it off and made me put it around my neck. "Wear it till Whiskers gets better. Please, Becky. I want you to."

"Yum! Can I come over?" said Michael that afternoon when we got home from school. The whole landing smelled of baking.

I said, "Maybe later." First I wanted to see how Whiskers was doing.

Mrs. Galloway called to me, "Come on in the kitchen, I saved you the beaters and bowl." She always does. She says I get them cleaner by licking than the dishwasher can.

But I went straight into my room, over to my bureau.

Whiskers was just the same. Quiet. Not purring. Even when I stroked and stroked her. And she wasn't thirsty. She wouldn't take a drop of milk. Or water, either.

"She will when she's ready," said Mrs. Galloway. "Cats know what's good for them."

Then the phone rang. "Hello, is this Becky?"

I didn't recognize the voice. Probably some salesman for who knows what. They're pretty tricky. They can find out the first names of who lives where from mailing lists and things like that. I got ready to slam the receiver down.

But then he said, "This is Pete. I hope I'm not disturbing you."

Yes, he was disturbing me!

"I just want to know how Whiskers is."

What's it to you, I nearly said.

Then he asked the dumbest thing. "What color are her gums?"

Purple with yellow stripes, I felt like saying. What color did he think?

I said, "They're pink."

So then he said I should go see if they were paler than usual.

I did. I couldn't tell.

Pete said, "That's okay. See you later, Becky. I've heard a lot about you, and I'm looking forward to meeting you."

I could hear him waiting for me to say, Same here. Well, he had a long wait coming. I just said, "Uh-huh," and I hung up.

It can really get you down sometimes when the phone rings and rings and rings and every time you think *this* time it'll be the person you really want to talk to. But it's not.

Kyra called. Then Melanie. They both asked, "How's Whiskers?"

Then Michael. "Can I come over now?"

No. I didn't want him to.

I thought, Come on, Dad, *you* call me. I'm not supposed to call him till after 6 o'clock when long-distance phone rates go down. I did anyway, but he wasn't there.

My father is terrific to talk to about subjects like Midnight Soup, and why there's snow on top of Mount Hood the whole year around, and how to draw waterfalls, thunder, roller coasters, things like that. Other things he clams up about. Like, for instance, how many kids I should be allowed to invite for sleep-overs. Or, if it's fair that Mom won't let me see movies she thinks are too gruesome that my friends have already seen three or four times. I don't even ask Dad things like that anymore. He'd just say, in a down tone of voice, Honey, that's between you and Mom.

He's no big expert on cats, and anyway what could he say from that far away? Still, I wanted to talk to him.

Mrs. Galloway went to a lot of trouble, slivering up vegetables. She made a dip, and a special sauce for the roast. She wanted dinner to be extra good.

And Mom had laid her new outfit on her bed, silk pants and a shimmery plum-color top, very pretty, ready to change into.

Well, at five past six, before she was even home yet, Pete arrived, with his doctor bag.

I have a bunch of tests I give to whoever goes out with Mom. The first is looks. They can't have black curly hair, or sparkly almost-black eyes like my father, or be *as* handsome. They should be a little good-looking, though. Pete is medium tall, with blond-brown hair and blue-green eyes. He passed the looks test okay.

The next test I give them is how many out

of the three most stupid questions do they ask me:

1) How do I like school?

2) What grade am I in?

3) What is my usual bedtime? (So they can start figuring how long till they get to be alone with Mom.)

Pete passed that test okay, too. The only question he asked was, "Where's Whiskers?"

Another test is how they act around cats. He'd already petted Debbie like somebody who's used to them, so I showed him Whiskers in the sweater drawer. "Better not touch her," I said.

So then he took the drawer by its side, and pulled it right out of the bureau. He moved it onto my bed. I was pretty surprised. He opened up his doctor bag and took out this little bitty stethoscope, half the size of a regular one. It looked like a toy one. And he listened to Whiskers' chest. He took her blood pressure, too.

I said, "Mom already did that." But he had a good touch, I had to admit.

He pushed Whiskers' upper lip back very gently. She didn't even mind. He said, "See those gums? They're not that pink."

It was true. Her gums were pale, almost white.

He handled her like he really knew what he was doing.

I asked, "Aren't you a G.P., same as Mom?" G.P. means general practitioner. "Are you also a vet?"

"Not 'also.' I'm a vet full time. I thought you knew."

No. Mom may have mentioned it when she first met him and I didn't pay attention. Or I forgot. Now that he'd told me, I was glad he was there.

So was Whiskers. Or at least she didn't mind, even when he held her eyelid up and took a good look at one eye. Then the other.

"Will she be okay?" I asked.

He said, "I hope so." He felt her belly. "Is she usually skinny or chubby?"

"Not skinny. Not chubby. Just right. What about her knee?"

"That's not a worry right now." Pete took her out of the drawer and held her in an odd way, with her head lower down than the rest of her.

"Why are you holding her like that?"

"To try to get the blood circulating better."

She shivered. I wrapped my blue angora sweater around her. Pete said, "Good, that should help to warm her."

Then I heard Mom's key in the lock. She came into my room with her coat still on.

She and Pete gave each other this special look. Like, they were so happy to see each other! That was the first thing, above everything else.

Then, quick, Mom came over to me, and took my face between her hands. Because she already knew, she'd read it in Pete's eyes, how things were with Whiskers.

Pete said in a quiet voice, "I think she's going into shock. From internal bleeding."

Mrs. Galloway was standing there with us. Mom thanked her for fixing such a wonderful dinner (she could tell from the smells). She said we'd have it when we got home.

I wrapped two more sweaters around Whiskers and we drove her to Montague Animal Hospital. Pete works there.

That was Friday evening.

Whiskers hardly ever gets to ride in the car. I was holding her, very steady, so she wouldn't feel any bumps. I wanted to talk to her, say things like, Look, over there's Prospect Park. And I'll take good care of Debbie while you're gone. And, You'll be home again in no time. I'm good at pretending all sorts of far-out, never-never things. But Whiskers was too out of it. Not exactly sleeping, but not awake, even though her eyes were a little bit open. Anyway, not even I could pretend that she'd want to hear about where Prospect Park is, or about Debbie, or about anything at all. I don't think she even knew where she was or who was holding her.

They took her straight into the X-ray room to try to see where she was bleeding inside. They brought her back out and didn't say, just that they might take more X-rays in the morning. Meantime, they'd watch her carefully.

She had to go in a cage, like the other sick animals. They let me put her in. But not with the sweaters around her. They said the heat was on, and she'd be warm enough.

Then we had to leave.

Pete put his arm around Mom. "I don't mean to brag, Naomi, but this place is the Mount Sinai of animal hospitals."

Mom smiled. She worked at Mount Sinai

one year. It's supposed to be a very good hospital, maybe the best in all of New York.

We were walking to the car. Pete started to put his other arm around me. I didn't say no, or shrug it off my shoulder. But I didn't want it there. He could tell. He took it away.

The Saddest Thing
That Ever Happened

I had a horrible dream. And the phone was ringing. Either for real or in the dream. I couldn't tell. I went back to sleep.

I woke up again. It was still dark out. I went to the bathroom. Then I saw a crack of light under Mom's door so I went in to her.

She was sitting up in bed. She got up and came to me. She had her beautiful lavender nightgown on with lace in front. She pulled me close to her. She put my face against the bony part of her chest. She said, "Oh, Becca!"

So then I knew.

The phone had really rung before. Pete called her up from the animal hospital. Whiskers was dead. She had died at 2 A.M. "In her sleep," Mom said.

Mom cried.

I figured I would, too. I moved my head away. I didn't want to get her nightgown even wetter. I usually cry a lot when anything even a little sad happens. This was the saddest thing that ever happened. Even sadder than when Dad moved away because I knew I'd see Dad again. The weird thing was, I didn't cry. Not one single tear.

"Come into my bed," Mom said.

I didn't want to.

I went to look for Debbie. She was on the couch in the living room. I took her into bed with me. I figured once I was lying down, holding her, I'd start crying buckets and somehow that would help.

Well, I lay there, stroking her, and she

started purring, like nothing was wrong. And my eyes stayed as dry as the desert.

Mom was supposed to be on duty today, Saturday. She got one of the other doctors to fill in for her. She had a date with Pete for this evening but she broke it. We put out enough food for Debbie for two days, and we drove to Syosset, Long Island, to Grandma Sonia's for the weekend.

I usually love it there. We did nice things, and Mom and Grandma Sonia were extra sweet to me.

But I couldn't enjoy anything. That was not the weird part. No, you wouldn't expect a person whose cat has just died to enjoy things right away. The weird part was that both those days I still didn't cry one single tear for Whiskers.

I felt like a robot walking on the beach. Like a robot picking apples. Like a robot going to the movies. Not like my usual self. And I got scared. What if not just Whiskers died, but all my feelings along with her?

Usually I tell things that scare me to Mom and it helps. But those whole two days I could almost not talk to Mom at all, much less tell her about this.

Monday morning, going to school, I told Michael, "Whiskers died."

He said, "Oh, that's terrible. Wow, Becky, you are brave."

Because I wasn't crying.

Oh, I wished I could feel brave. Instead of all empty and dry.

When I got into our classroom, Kyra was waiting for me by the cubbies. And somehow, just seeing her there made the weirdness start to get less.

One look at my face, and she came running to me with her arms out.

I undid the clasp of the necklace with the four-leaf clover she lent me.

"No. You keep it, Becky. Even if it didn't bring luck. It's still pretty, don't you think? Please. I want you to have it."

So I put it back on.

Then Melanie came. The three of us sat in the corner back near the cubbies. I told them the whole story. And I cried my eyes out. I was so relieved!

It wasn't true that my feelings had died. I was filled with feelings. They came pouring out of me, to Kyra and to Melanie. "Oh, Mel, oh, Kyra, it's so unfair! She was so healthy and so beautiful, I loved her so, so much!"

That's when Jason Abeloff came to his cubby, wearing his Dracula shirt.

Oh, Mom,
if You Only Knew . . .

"Gosh, Becky," said Jason, "that sounds tragic. *T-R-A-G-I-C*." He spelled it out, just as a little reminder that he once won a spelling bee with that word in it.

"Hey, this is a private conversation," Kyra said.

"Excuse me. I was just trying to be nice."

"Look," said Kyra in a fierce voice, "her cat died. So just kindly leave us alone, okay?"

"Right, butt out," I said.

"Okay, okay, I'm sorry," said Jason. "It's just the way you sounded, Becky, I thought it was your mom, or somebody—"

That's when things got blurry. Like when I'm not wearing my glasses. And this picture came on, bright and sharp, in my mind: Mom dead, Whiskers still alive. Before I knew it, red stuff, blood, ran down Jason Abeloff's face onto the Dracula shirt. And there stood Ms. Field, our teacher.

So then she kept me in for recess. And I couldn't write the explanation, and drew the tree instead.

When I came home that afternoon, Mrs. Galloway tried to be extra nice to me. She fixed my favorite snacking sandwich: peanut butter and sliced pickle on pumpernickel bread. And for once she didn't say *she* wouldn't be caught dead, eating one of those.

Usually she pours my milk into any old glass. But Monday she looked around for the glass I really like, the one with daisies painted on it. I found it in a garage sale out near

Grandma's. It was one of a kind. I could never find another one like it.

Debbie was lying curled up on my chair. Any other day Mrs. G. would have picked her up roughly, or just shoved her down. That day she said, "Pardon me, Debbie," in a nice voice and lifted her up gently, so I could sit down. Then she put her in my lap. "There. Aren't you glad you've still got her?"

Yes, I was. Debbie's not much of a lap cat, though. She jumped down right away.

One reason I loved that glass was that the daisies on it looked exactly like the ones on the blue-velvet armchair in our foyer where Mom and I sit when we have our special time together.

For once, instead of looking forward to that time all afternoon, I dreaded it. I didn't want to have it. Because Mom would guess that something happened in school. And she'd want to talk about it.

Mrs. Galloway said, "It's not the end of the world yet. Go on, drink your milk."

I took my eyeglasses off. I just felt like taking a little rest from everything looking so sharp and clear. I looked at the milk in the daisy glass, its velvety whiteness. And I thought of a googol. A googol is the number ten with one hundred zeros after it. I multiplied the milk by a googol in my mind. That way it turned into the Milky Way . . .

"Tsk, tsk." Mrs. G. clucked her tongue. "Time to quit moping. You may not think so now, Reb, but you'll get over it."

No, never, I swore.

She moved the glass closer to me.

I lowered my head to it. Quick, before Mrs. G. could stop me, I stuck my tongue into the glass and lapped up milk Whiskers' way. In Whiskers' memory.

Just then the phone rang. Dad—I still hadn't talked to him. I needed to, so badly! This time it had to be Dad! I almost already heard him say, Becky-Boo, is that you? I lunged for the phone. The glass got knocked over.

"Hi there, Becky," said Mrs. Galloway's husband. "Could I speak to my ever-loving wife?"

She was on the floor, picking up pieces of glass. I got down, picked some up, too.

"Don't! You'll cut yourself to smithereens!" She grabbed the receiver and waved me away.

I went into my room. I sat and looked at the picture of the Brooklyn Bridge over my desk. It's by my father. He's a painter, and he's really good. He painted that picture when he still lived with us, before he and Mom got divorced. I wished it were a real bridge, not just to Manhattan, but all the way west, and that I could walk across it, all the way to Portland. Or else, up into the sky . . .

My fingers felt like drawing. I sharpened a pencil to a fine point. And I started. First, a cat. Then two stars at its ears. Then another cat, more stars, and another, and another. Drawing cats is easy, once you know how. Stars are even easier.

I drew some of the cats' tails high in the air, and some cats' tails held low. I tried to make the low ones look as though the cats were swinging them, but that was hard to do. I gave some cats folded-up wings, and other cats open wings. I let some of them fly from star to star. Then I drew harps between some cats' paws. Also, violins, flutes, drums, cymbals. The cymbals came out looking wrong, so I changed them to cellos. Pretty soon the cats who weren't flying around were playing all the musical instruments I could think of that were not too hard to draw: trumpets, oboes, clarinets, triangles, even a piano.

I started to run out of space. But I didn't want to stop yet. So I sharpened my pencil to a finer point, and drew more cats, smaller and smaller. A little bit the way they're drawn on the most crowded pages of *Millions of Cats*. When I got to the edges of the paper, I drew them as tiny as baby mosquitoes. The tinier, the farther away from Earth they were, billions and trillions of miles away, a googol miles away . . .

I'd left a little space at the bottom, and I wrote the name of the picture there: CAT HEAVEN, THE MILKY WAY.

Then I imagined what people would think of it.

Mrs. Galloway: Dumb idea. Animals don't go to Heaven.

Mom: Poor Becca. And she'd feel even sorrier for me that I miss Whiskers so much.

Michael: What a stupid picture. There's no such place!

No, of course not. I balled it up and dropped it in my wastebasket.

Christians don't believe that animals go to Heaven. Jews don't believe in any Heaven up in the sky. Melanie says her father says that Heaven can be right here on earth while you're still alive. I guess he means when you're feeling really happy. I couldn't imagine feeling that way ever again. What I *could* imagine was tomorrow morning. Going to Mr. Bruzzo's office. Hell. That may be a swear word, but it tells just how I felt.

So then be reasonable, I told myself, and got my pen, and took a piece of notebook paper.

WHY I PUNCHED JASON ABELOFF IN THE

NOSE, I wrote across the top.

I explained that he ducked. That's how come I got him in the nose. I only meant to punch him on the arm. Because he said— But I couldn't write that down in a million years! I could sooner have walked to Portland, Oregon, on my father's painted bridge! Just thinking about it brought the picture back to my mind. All those graves . . . Mom, oh, Mom, if you knew!

My door opened. It was only five-fifteen. But there she stood, with a sad, sweet Mom-smile that shot through me like an arrow.

Things were quiet so she'd left work early. "I wanted to be with my Becca," she said. And she held out her arms for a hug.

We always hug when she comes home. But I couldn't. One reason was, if I got up from my desk, she might see WHY I PUNCHED JASON. I tore it up and threw it away.

Mom came over and put her arms around me from behind. I made myself sit very still and not lean my head against her. I thought, Oh, Mom, if you only knew what I imagined in that picture in my mind, you wouldn't want to hug me.

Mom asked, "What was that you tore up?"

"Um, nothing. Just some homework."

She asked me to come sit in our blue chair with the daisies for our private time together.

"I can't, Mom. I have to do that homework over."

"All right, when you're done, then."

I'd never be done! But I said, "All right."

She went out of my room.

I put my head on my desk and just sat like that, trying to think of nothing. I guess I fell asleep. Because next thing, Mom was saying, "Dinner's nearly ready. Aren't we going to sit together a little while tonight?"

"No. I'm still not done."

"Well, all right." Mom sounded a little bit hurt. "I guess there are times when everybody needs to be alone. I can understand that."

No, no, no, that wasn't why! Mom didn't understand at all! And there was no way—no way!—I could explain it.

"I'll call you when dinner's ready," she said and she left me alone.

At dinner she asked, "Now do you want to talk?"

"Uh-uh."

"Okay, I guess you will when you're ready to."

We hardly ever watch TV while we eat. But she turned on the news. "You don't mind, do you, Becca?"

No, I didn't mind. Not till the commercial came on. It was for 9 Lives. I'd seen it hundreds of times. I know it's meant to be cute, just a joke. But it got me mad. I jabbed the knob that switches off the set.

"Hey!" said Mom. "You're not the only person in this dining alcove. I live here, too." She switched the set back on. Morris the cat's snooty voice came back on.

I stuck my fingers in my ears. I shouted, "I hate the name of that cat food. Nine lives is such a lie! Cats have *one* life, that's all."

"Of course," said Mom. "I didn't make it

up, so don't blame me. And while you're feeling sorry for yourself, just remember: You're not the only one who misses Whiskers. I miss her, too, you know."

"I *do* blame you." I hadn't meant to say that. It just slipped out.

Mom put her fork down. "How do you mean?"

"It's because you're so crazy about that guy Pete—!" Such a look came over her face. I was sorry I'd started. But now that I had, I couldn't stop. "I blame Pete too! Why didn't he come right away?"

"He was on duty," Mom said. "He takes care of other animals too, you know—"

"I don't care! If that hospital where he works is such a great place, why didn't he make them operate on Whiskers?"

Mom gave me all kinds of reasons. No veterinary surgeon was there, the operating room was closed. Besides, operations can't do magic.

I don't know what all else. "I don't want to hear about it! I just blame him, that's all. I hate Pete. I hope he—"

Mom put her hand over my mouth.

I pushed her hand away. And I left the table.

"Rebecca Suslow, you come back here."

I ran out of the dining alcove. I thought, Good, now she's mad at me. That made it easier than when she was being so sweet.

Later, when I was in bed, she came into my room. She said, "I want you to understand, it wasn't Pete's fault. He did everything he could. I'm sure you really know that. It wasn't anyone's fault. How about making up now?"

Oh, I wanted to!

But I turned and faced the wall. I thought, If Mom knew what I imagined, *she'd* be the one who wouldn't want to make up with *me*. I thought, And tomorrow she'll want to even less, when Mr. Bruzzo calls her up and makes her come to school.

Mr. "Brute" Bruzzo

Sometimes, when everything's too awful, you go to sleep and forget everything. When I woke up next morning, sunshine shone in through my curtains. I thought, Today'll be a nice day. Then everything crashed down on top of me: Whiskers dead. Punching Jason. Blood running down his face. Ms. Field sending me to Mr. Bruzzo. Mr. Bruzzo sending for Mom. I crawled back under my covers.

"No written explanation, Becky? Well, then, here's a hall pass. Off you go," said Ms. Field.

Everybody in the class knew where to. Everybody thought, Wow, I'm glad I'm not Becky Suslow.

In a little room outside the principal's office sits the secretary of the school, Mrs. Hollinger. She said, "Mr. Bruzzo stepped out for a few minutes. Go ahead in. Sit down and wait for him."

I sat very straight in the chair across from his desk. My heart bumped around in my chest.

His office faces the same way our classroom does. The window was open. I could see the playground tree, and I could hear sparrows making noise in it.

I was scared. Who wouldn't be, waiting for Mr. "Brute"? But an even bigger reason why my heart bumped was the picture in my mind. There it was again, and me in it, almost more than where I really was.

Tall trees, green grass, gray gravestones. One grave open. In front of it, Rabbi Rosen, in his rabbi clothes. Me next to him. Holding a handful of dirt. I'm supposed to throw it in. And everybody's there. All the kids in my class. All Mom's friends. And guess who else: Dad. Well, naturally. Both arms around me.

Then, in the next part of the picture, the funeral's over. Dad and I open the door to our apartment. And two cats come to greet us. Debbie and Whiskers. Whiskers is still alive!

The me in the picture was just about to pick her up, hug and squeeze and kiss her. *Clomp, clomp*, into where I really was, came Mr. Bruzzo, the principal. His footsteps shook the floor.

He boomed, "Hello. I haven't seen you in here before. You must be a first-time offender. What's your name? Whose class are you in? What brings you to this dreaded torture chamber?"

It felt like one, all right.

And his nickname, "Brute," fit him all right too. He has a long, bony face. His jaw juts out and his nose is long and bent-down like a buffalo's, with big nostrils with hair growing out of them. He has bushy eyebrows, and moose-brown eyes. I couldn't decide which he looked like more, a moose or a buffalo.

I told him my name and class. "I'm here because I punched somebody." I looked down at his giant-sized shoes. I could feel him looking at me.

"Whom did you punch?"

"A boy in my class. Jason Abeloff."

He asked me the question I knew was coming. "What for?"

"Because, um—," was all I could say.

"How hard did you punch him?"

"Pretty hard," I told the giant shoes. "He got a nosebleed. He bled all over his shirt."

"In that case, you've already taken care of punishing him. I won't need to punish him more. So you needn't worry about 'telling' on him. But I do need to know what he did that made you so mad. You can either tell me now, or—" He swiveled around in his chair. He opened a file drawer marked *S*. He took out

my folder, read things in it. "Or, you can tell me all about it when your mother comes to school. I see she's a busy woman." He swiveled back around to me. "I suggest you tell me *now*."

You don't sit in that chair facing Mr. Bruzzo and *not* try to do what he suggests. I started, "Well, you see, my cat died. I was talking about her with two friends of mine, Kyra Farris and Melanie Rosen, when Jason—"

"Hold it right there. Talk to *me* about her." Mr. Bruzzo asked me things like what was her name, how did I get her, how long did I have her, how did I feel about her, and what did she die from. I was surprised. I never thought a principal would want to know things like that.

The whole time I answered, he kept his eyes on my face. I mostly looked down at my lap or at the floor, just once or twice back at his face. And it didn't remind me that much of a moose or buffalo anymore.

I got to the part where Jason butted in.

"And Jason said I made it sound so tragic, he thought a *person* died."

Mr. Bruzzo asked, "Did he say *what* person?"

"Mm-hmm." I looked away.

"Who?"

I made up my mind to say it. What did I have to lose? The picture was already there in my mind, as real as could be, I could see it when I shut my eyes, as sharp as on TV. I said, "My mother." I put my head down on my knees.

Mr. Bruzzo asked, "Are you ashamed?"

Yes, and how! Not of the business with Jason. Just of the picture, and that it wouldn't go away. So ashamed, so ashamed, I felt like never looking up again, and as if there couldn't be anyone else alive on earth as horrible as me.

Mr. Bruzzo gave me a lecture about what if everybody in the school punched out everybody else any time they felt like it. There'd be long lines of people waiting to get into the nurse's office. There'd have to be a shuttle bus to the nearest hospital. Nobody'd learn anything, except about punching, and about ducking out of the way. The place would be a madhouse. Didn't I agree?

"Yes."

Well, then would I please promise never to punch people in school again, no matter how much they deserved it?

Yes, I promised, and started to stand up. I thought he was letting me go.

"Wait. I'm not through with you yet." He reached into a desk drawer. "Take a look at this."

He handed me a photograph, not in color. It looked faded. It was of a big turtle and an old-fashioned kid with a very short haircut and pants that stopped at the knees.

He said, "That was me. I was around your age. That was my turtle, Methuselah. I gave him that name because I hoped he'd live to a hundred or more. He lived a very healthy life. He ate every kind of lettuce. Iceberg was his favorite. And he put away good-sized portions of hamburger, cooked or raw. He had free run of the apartment. He took baths in the bathtub, and naps and long sleeps under our beds.

"Well, one day I came home from softball practice. My mother looked like she'd been crying. She said, 'Oh, Luigi (that's Louis in Italian), something bad happened.'

"I said, 'No!' I started to cry. My dad had been in the hospital with a case of pneumonia for a week. I held on to my mother. And—" Mr. Bruzzo leaned across the desk and asked me in a low voice, "Want to know what I prayed?"

Sure, I wanted to know.

"'Please, God, don't let anything have happened to my turtle.' Well, touch wood—," he touched the side of the desk, "my father got better and came home. He's in the pink, to this day."

"And Methuselah?" I asked, even though I already kind of knew the answer.

"He died. It's still very vivid in my mind. So I can understand what you're going through over Whiskers."

For a moment both of us were quiet. Then he said, "Do me a favor, please: Keep that Methuselah story to yourself. It's kind of personal."

Yes, I could understand that.

He stood up. "Okay, now go on back to your classroom. Tell Ms. Field as far as I'm concerned the matter is closed." He shook a warning finger at me. "But you'd better watch that fast fist of yours from now on." His voice was back to booming. But as I was going out the door, he gave me a human-to-human smile, and I gave one back to him.

Portrait of Whiskers

"Well, thank goodness, you're looking less down in the dumps," said Mrs. Galloway when I came home that afternoon. "Has the end of the world been postponed?" And she handed me a package—postmarked Portland! "Here, this came in the mail, for you."

I ripped it open. Inside was a box of Artrue markers, eight of them: red, blue, orange, purple, yellow, green, black, and white. Also a big art pad, almost poster size. And a note:

Dear Becky-Boo,

I've been working with markers like this lately. They're terrific. Hope you like them, too.

Ninety kisses, a hundred hugs,
Your Dad-O.

I tried the colors right away. They go on easily and smoothly. They glow, almost like oil paints that real artists use, but they don't smudge into each other. And the paper is the kind where you can work right on the pad and the color doesn't bleed through from one sheet to the next. (Bleed is the word artists use for when that happens.) I dabbed and doodled, made designs of different color circles, stripes, dots, flowers, and faces.

Then Debbie came into my room. Debbie has Whiskers' coloring: black with pretty much the same white places. But the way she moves, like she's doing dance steps, is different. I wished I could make a drawing of that.

She hopped up on my windowsill and

looked out. I got busy with the pad and marker. Sitting still is easier to draw than motion. I didn't get very far. In a minute she hopped down.

"Hop back up there, Debbie, please."

She narrowed her eyes at me, sort of like saying, I don't understand what you want me to do. But I think she understood all right, she just didn't feel like it.

I said, "Come over here, then."

She came, for a quick snuggle, then ran out of my door. She's always on the go.

I felt like working with the markers. I turned to the next sheet on the pad. I used the black marker again. I just let my hand travel along the paper with it, any way it wanted to. Out came a curved line—the start of what? I didn't know yet. Then a *V*, upside down. And another, shorter line, another upside-down *V*. Like two ears sticking up. It started to be a cat face. Not any cat face in particular. Just any old ordinary cat face.

Then I got this huge, enormous longing all

the way through me, and I didn't know what to do.

I stood up and walked around my room. I stopped in front of my bureau. I opened up my sweater drawer wide. I bent down and put my face in. I laid my cheek against the blue angora sweater and stayed like that for a while.

Then I brought the pad and marker over, and I stood there and drew the bureau drawer, what it looks like when you look down into it. It was the hardest thing. I used up three sheets of the pad. Finally it started to look like a drawer, but not big enough. So I turned the pad on its side and started over, using the whole width of the paper.

Next, I needed a pencil. I went and sharpened one. I sat down on the floor with my back against the bureau. I held the pad on my knees. I closed my eyes and concentrated, concentrated. Then I drew a cat lying in the drawer. Not sick and hurt, just snuggling in there with the sweaters.

Most of my pencils have chewed-off erasers. Luckily this one's eraser was still on. I needed it. I had to erase a lot. Finally the ears matched, the eyes were wide enough apart, and the tail curled under just right.

I took the drawing over to my desk and used the markers for filling in the colors. Black—it went on silky smooth—for most of the fur. White for under the chin, for the paws and tail tip. There wasn't a pink marker. So I used a pink crayon for the mouth and the insides of the ears.

The green-golden eyes were the hardest to do. The best part was the eyebrows sticking up and the long white whisker hairs curving down. Those were easy. Those were fun.

When it was finished, I went and showed it to Mrs. Galloway. She was surprised. "Hey, look at that! When did you get to be such a good artist?"

The only thing she criticized was where I'd put the title. "You put it too far over to the right." She thinks titles of pictures should be smack in the middle.

So instead of calling it just WHISKERS, I changed it to BECKY SUSLOW'S WHISKERS. That brought the whole thing closer to the center.

It Will Always
Be There

That night Mom had a date with Pete. But they were going to meet at a restaurant, instead of him coming here to pick her up. Mom figured I wouldn't feel too much like seeing him. She figured right!

So I thought she'd get home late, and I'd probably be asleep. But at six-fifteen, her usual time, she walked in.

"Mom! You're home! How come? Aren't you going out with Pete?"

"Yes, later. There's something I need to do first."

"What?"

We were standing in the foyer. She pointed to the armchair. "Sit there with you for a while."

"*You* need to?"

"Sure. Did you think you were the only one?"

I'd never thought of it like that.

So we sat there for our private time—which I hadn't even expected!

She asked, "What kind of day has it been?"

"Well, it started out bad—"

She laid her cheek next to mine. "You mean because when you woke up you remembered about Whiskers?"

"Yes. And something else, too: I had to go to Mr. Bruzzo's office today."

Mom sat up. "You did?"

"Don't get upset, Mom. It's okay. It wasn't as bad as I thought. Mr. Bruzzo was pretty understanding. And you don't have to come to school about it."

"'It?' What's 'it?' What did you do?"

"Well, yesterday I punched this kid in my class, you don't know him, Jason Abeloff—"

"That doesn't sound like you. How come?"

"Well, Melanie, Kyra and I were talking, and he came over, he butted in. He said—"

Mom, waited. Then she said, "It must have been something really bad."

"It was. Listen, Mom, would it be okay if I don't tell it to you?"

Mom had her arms around me. We sat close together. She said, "Yes, it would be okay. There are always things people don't tell each other. Even people who love each other as much as you and I do."

"That's what I think, too." All of a sudden, I felt good, all the way through me. I'd started to think I'd never feel like that again. I guess Mom felt that way, too.

"Mom! Wait till you see the present I got today, terrific art markers, and—"

Debbie came dancing into the foyer. I picked her up onto our laps. I got her to lie still for a minute. Then she leaped down andstarted cleaning herself, licking her fur even shinier and smoother.

Mom said, "I have to go 'beautify' myself, too." She likes that word, she thinks it's funny.

I said, "You're beautiful already, Mom. Wait, don't get up yet, I want to show you something."

I went to get the picture. But when I looked at it, I wasn't satisfied with the title. Not because it was off center. That's not so important.

The picture came into my mind of when we first saw Whiskers, Mom and me, up on the roof of our building. It was summertime. We'd gone up to water some plants Mom kept there. And this great looking cat came out from behind one of the chimneys. She came over to *both* of us.

So Mom's name belonged in the title, too. I put it in, right over my name:

BECKY AND NAOMI SUSLOW'S WHISKERS

Mom drew in her breath. "Oh, Becca!" She looked at it for the longest time. I could tell she liked it.

Now it's framed. Mom took it to the frame shop Dad and some artist friends of his used. The frame is black with tiny flecks of gold.

We hung it in the foyer. Sometimes, when we're sitting together, we look at it. And every day when I come home from school, it's there.

ABOUT THE AUTHOR

In addition to writing children's books Doris Orgel works as a translator and reviewer of children's books. She received The Child Study Award for her YA novel *The Devil in Vienna*. She lives in New York City.

ABOUT THE ILLUSTRATOR

Carol Newsom is the illustrator of *My War with Mrs. Galloway* (Viking Kestrel and Puffin). She lives in Colorado.